The Berenstain Bears®
GET THE
GROUCHIES

Stan & Jan Berenstain

inchworm
PRESS
™

Most of the time things went pretty smoothly in the big tree house down a sunny dirt road deep in Bear Country. The members of the Bear Family got along pretty well together.

They smiled at each other
more often than not.

They took turns in the bathroom.

They usually
passed the honey
when asked. They
even said "please"
and "thank you"
most of the time.

But one day things were different at the big tree house. Maybe it was because the day wasn't sunny.

Or maybe it was because the Bears didn't have a good night's sleep.

But whatever the reason, they all woke up with a terrible case of the grouchies. It was as though the whole family got up on the wrong side of the bed.

Not only did they not take turns in the bathroom, they grumped and grouched about who was going to get to the bathroom first.

And while Papa, Mama, and Brother grumped and grouched, Sister sneaked in ahead of them and locked the door.

That's when Papa, Mama, and Brother really got grouchy. They not only grumped and grouched, they knocked and banged.

Wow! Talk about the grouchies!
Talk about a racket!

It woke up the night owl who had just
managed to fall asleep.

It woke up the night crawler who had just
come in from a hard night of crawling.

It woke up the bats who had just fallen asleep after a long night of chasing bugs.

And breakfast was worse.
They hogged the honey.

They reached across
the table.

They snarled and sneered at each other.

As a matter of fact they sneered and snarled through the whole day.

They fought about little things like who would
answer the phone when it rang.

They fought about big things like which television show they would watch.

It was terrible! It was awful! But most of all *it was exhausting!*

By bedtime the Bear Family was completely exhausted. The grouchies had worn them out.

As they sat around being grouchy,
they looked at each other.

When Mama saw how miserable
Papa, Brother and Sister looked,
she couldn't help smiling.

Then Brother smiled.

Then Papa.

Then Sister.

Mama learned a lesson that day.
She learned there's nothing like a
smile to get rid of the grouchies.

"How about some milk and honey
before we go to bed?" said Mama.

After milk and honey . . .

and yawns all around,

the Bears said good-night to each other, good-bye to the grouchies, and went to bed.

When they woke up the next morning everything was back to normal at the big tree house down a sunny dirt road deep in Bear Country.